Between the Stalls:

A Journey with Horses, Life, and Relationships

Between the Stalls:

A Journey with Horses, Life, and Relationships

Allison James

First Printing: 2017

ISBN 978-1-365-85157-5

Snickers Publications
2604-B El Camino Real, #282
Carlsbad, CA 92008

Contents

Introduction

As I enter the "twilight" years of my life, I marvel at the chances I've had to meet many people and make lasting friendships through horses. I reflect on how being rescued myself while at a horse rescue organization, I learned how deep a relationship humans can have with their equine friends. Horses heal, horses are magical!

I was a three-year-old when I got the "bug" for horses. I couldn't leave my parents alone a day without asking for a horse. Not a pony! I wanted a HORSE. I had horse toys, played horse, drew horses, watched horses on TV and movies. There was no end to how much horse I could get into my system.

As a teen, I took every chance I could to find a way to ride horses. My parents were not wealthy and they considered riding a "wealthy person's activity" therefore, no riding lessons were in our budget. They threw a few lessons at me to appease me and keep me busy while they were doing other things like playing bridge or watching my brothers play baseball. The lessons weren't consistent enough to do more than allow me to sit on a horse in a trail ride or take off in a gallop in the arena when I could sneak it in while renting one of the horses at a local barn. I envied all the girls whose mothers cheered them on from the arena rails during their weekly lessons.

Finally, in my twenties with a year-old toddler of my own, we moved to an area of Los Angeles where there was a barn close by. Little did I know I was learning Dressage. I must have had a trainer who was out of place at the little western type barn where we were but she put me on that mare with a double bridle and yelled, “use your corners”, “change your diagonal”, “straight to A and down the center line”, “half halt!” I didn’t know any better. I had no clue! I just wanted to ride. We had little shows just for the trainer and her students. Nothing fancy, no real judge. I got busy with my career and raising my child and eventually stopped riding….for THIRTY MORE YEARS!

After making a career and raising my daughter, I lost that “big corporate job”. Suddenly and not so nicely. I lost my home, had to file bankruptcy and found myself single at an older age with no one looking to hire me. I went back to ‘zero’. Some of you recognize this state. It’s when you must tell yourself to put one foot in front of the other each day. You wake up with what feels like a pit in your stomach where your identity used to be. You reach way down deep and ask probing questions. Who am I? What do I like to do? Where do I go from here? What will become of me now? Enter horses – again!

Having time off and trying to "discover or reinvent myself", I took a course on energy work with animals. I was always somewhat a "sensitive" (sensing/hearing spirit and having some telepathic or psychic experiences as a child). The instructor had us go to a local barn to work on horses. There I was, in my element!

I reached out shortly thereafter to a rescue organization nearby to offer my new-found healing services. Just so happens, they had a sick horse. I got caught up in the work, but even more, learned about the actual caretaking of horses. While riding in my twenties, there was the horse, all tacked up ready to go. No real grooming had to be done, just hop on and ride and someone else put the horse up. Here at the rescue, we mucked stalls, handled the horses, groomed, fed, administered meds and even got to ride them bareback occasionally. I was at once in HEAVEN! While there were many personalities to work with between all the volunteers and the ranch owner (horse people all have "personalities"), there was a bonding that went on as we all shared the love of the horses, the hard and sweaty work of caretaking and rescuing of these majestic animals. I made note that it seemed many of the women were in their 50's like me. We all had done our child raising/careers and now had some time on our hands to return to our first love – horses.

I had never owned a horse of my own. My three-year-old was coming out in me again. I HAD to have a horse! Now it seemed possible since I knew a bit more about how to care for them. But without a job and no real income, it seemed impossible financially. I would have to just settle for these rescued lovelies!

Finally, the unemployment stopped and I found myself with an ideal situation. A job that was flexible enough for me to work from home, make my own hours and have a decent wage even though it was half of what I made in the past. I finally had that "work/life balance" that everyone strives for. The universe works in this way if you've noticed. It brings to you what you focus on! I was so focused on horses, they just came my way. I was sitting on the couch one day after having left the rescue ranch, missing the horses and wanting to ride again. I perused the internet for a local riding barn. There it was – obscure but right down the street! How had I not known there were horses right under my nose all this time so close by! I put it off. I thought maybe I'd be too busy with my new job and would not have the time. I could not help but feel the pounding of a finger on my shoulder, prodding me. Spirit was at work here and persistent they were! "CALL THEM" was shouted into my psychic ear.

Ok, Ok, I answered.

Preface

I decided to write this book in honor of the horses and especially Snickers but to also share the deep relationships and bonding women have through our horse experiences. In our 50's, 60's and yes even into our 70's, we are bonded to each other through our horses. If we are not with the horses, we are talking about our horses (our non-horse friends cringe when we get together!). We shop for our horses and trade stories of horse tales. There is an automatic bond between us. We share ourselves deeply and support each other as a "sisterhood" of sorts. Like teenagers, we can talk for hours on the phone about horses and yes, even a bit of gossip of the barn goings on.

There must be something in our blood. Some sort of destiny for us to be together. This "sisterhood" of sorts must have a meaning. We raised our children, we had our careers, we've had our divorces (or two), never married, or had other persuasions. It doesn't matter. We love each other and we support each other like a village. It's therapy of sorts. We forget everything while on a horse.

We let the horse speak to our spirit nature from their huge hearts. We are a herd. And just maybe we find change is good...

Change, Nothing Stays the Same

Grooming Snickers was always a challenge. He came from an unknown place, starving, angry and misunderstood. My way with this old cast-away horse was cautious but firm. He paces, stops, pushes and generally just gets in your space. I knew he was not respecting me or anyone else. Here he was, this old thirty-something year old majestic bay with two white socks and a blaze, prancing with head high, tail fanned and dragon snorts every few footfalls. Getting him calm would be difficult today. His favorite mare was over in her pen and as far as he was concerned way too far away for his liking. Moving his feet was the only way to get his attention so I went and got the lunge whip and entered the round pen. He barely looks at me and keeps on prancing away running dangerously close. I move slowly to the middle of the round pen with my head down, making small gestures with a quiet mind and the whip behind me on the ground. I swish my feet and make my "awe shucks" look. He eventually has a curious moment as to what I'm looking at on the ground and stops. I look at him but with a sideways glance to his shoulder. He moves ever so slightly. I take a step toward his shoulder and raise the whip slightly beside me toward his flank. BAM! There he goes! Exploding into his prancing snorting panic around the round pen, I've lost him again. I again adjust my body to a slump, staying in the middle while he lunges himself. With an inner and outer calm demeanor. I say "ok, bud, I've got all day if you do" and again go into my "awe shucks" shuffle of my feet. The round pen floor appearing to be very intriguing, he eventually stops and looks. I notice his softer eye and more intention on me. We go again, the dance of moving feet. I move toward his shoulder and ever so slightly look at his flank. There! A slow move around me. I send him off to a walk. He bows his head and blows out. Calmness at last...

After walking, trotting and a few steps of canter in each direction, I get him to "hook on" and walk toward me. I approach him with the grooming kit, grabbing the curry and body brush, we begin. He has only been groomed infrequently and his owner is too afraid to pick up his feet so he was only handled by the Ferrier every six weeks or so this past few years. I fell in love with this horse a few months back. He and I just connected somehow even through his angry demeanor. I still have a hard time reaching for his head as I groom, he pulls back away each time but over time he's been getting a bit softer as I don't give up on him. Picking up his feet, he still plays with me on his left front refusing to pick it up. I'm awkward, not knowing how to get him to release his foot up. We tussle a bit with my consternation growing, his stubbornness increases and I sense him laughing inside at my attempts. Ah, treats are his motivation! I show him my pocket full of carrot pieces, reach once more for his foot and alas, it comes up! Treat delivered. We both win! .

As I continue to groom, he is enjoying the sun on his body, baking his old bones. It is a rhythmic movement as my right hand curries and my left hand swipes with the body brush. Crunch, crunch, swipe, Crunch, crunch, swipe, his tail moves ever so slightly and his body is slowing rocking to the rhythm of the brushes. I am in deep thought of nothing really. Suddenly I "hear" (inside my head more than an outside speaking) "Change, nothing stays the same". I jump a bit more alert. I know this "inside voice" from before. I've had some encounters with the "otherworld". Call it spirit or telepathic/psychic experiences, it is familiar. Snickers just spoke to me! We connected somehow in our hum of connected grooming enjoyment deep in thought of nothingness.

That's a curious statement I thought. My mind certainly didn't make it up. It had to come from him. What could it mean? **"Change, nothing stays the same"?**

Dark

It was a long time since a human had entered. The smell of his urine and the sting to his eyes was making him squint. He could feel the flies attacking his eyes and they were crunchy when he blinked and itching from the pus. There was some small amount of grass left on the floor. He was too tired to try and pick it up. His bones ached, his feet hurt and he lost interest in trying to look outside. The noise of the other horses was not a comfort. They whinnied their cry of help, loneliness and hunger. Like him, they were in their dark damp cold stalls. How long had it been? Maybe three days since he ate. He had water but it was green and smelled putrid. It was the only way to stay alive he told himself as he drank.

"GET!" The door to the barn flew open and the man yelled coming in. He kicked the dog that was standing by the door and the dog cowered and yelped, slinking off to the side. Light entered the barn for the first time in days. It hurt his eyes.

He squinted, pushing the pus and the flies out of his eye sockets. His coat was dirty and he was cold as he could feel there wasn't much flesh left on his bones. He wasn't even sure he was hungry anymore. He was just tired. He had no will to be there, to be anywhere really. He feared the man but he was too tired to move.

"Well, aren't you all lucky today!" the man said with a sneer to his voice. The truck will be here soon. I've finally got them to come and get you all out of my sight you old good for nothing eating machines!". The man smelled of liquor and cigarettes and sweat. He had barely left enough food for any of the horses and they saw him only every couple of days or so. He was mean and hit them sometimes. There were times where he brought a woman with him who seemed softer and pleaded with him to please "feed these poor rescued souls more food". He laughed at her and tossed his head. "These horses? They've seen their day. No one wants them. They are of no use other than for slaughter and dog food."

The rumble of a large truck could be heard in the distance. It made the floor shake a bit and hurt his feet even more. The sound was not a welcome sound. It made him uneasy. The stall was cold and dark but it was familiar. What would it be like to be in that truck? How will all the other horses react? Will I be stomped on? Kicked? Bitten?

With a deep sadness, he knew the destination of the truck would be final.

The man made his way to his stall last. Halter on, he was prodded and kicked until he finally moved his sore feet and his aching bones. With a last attempt at freedom and resistance he tried to rear, kick or bolt away from the man. It angered the man and he hit him. “You GET! You old sack of bones!” He looked at the truck and beyond. He developed enough energy from anger toward the man and drew on everything he had deep in his will and quickly opened his mouth and bit the man in the arm as hard as he could and then bolted out around the truck and down the road as he found his way to the next barnyard pasture.

The man angrily grabbed his arm as he stared at Snickers running away. “Awe, to heck with him” the man scowled as he collected his money from the truck driver while holding his now swollen arm. He’s a “goner” anyway. He won’t last long over there before he becomes pasture fodder. Snickers looked back as he hid behind a tree in the pasture. He was weak and breathing heavy but he was relieved to be away and no one was coming after him. He didn’t have to get in that awful truck.

He lay down in the shade of the tree, exhausted, he slept and dreamt. Kids laughing and riding him in the arena and in the outdoor area where they took him on trails which was his favorite. At the wash rack, they fussed over his beautiful shiny brown coat, black mane and tail and strong legs with two white stockings that tapered down to healthy hooves. He jumped over the poles and cavalettis and they laughed and cheered him on. Good Boy Snickers! He was the best horse the barn had for their riding program.

All Chaos Breaks Loose

The woman cautiously approached the horse in her pasture. "Well, well, where on earth did you come from?". She noticed his dull coat, fly bitten eyes and his wasting away. Wow, it was a wonder he was alive. Snickers eyed her with caution as well. Humans had not done well to him lately. He raised his head and snorted as much as he could. He felt his chest heave. It was all he could do to make himself bigger and scarier with all his might. She laughed. "Well, you do have spirit that's for sure!". She slowly walked toward him with an extended hand. "Hey, you are lucky my guys weren't out here grazing". Her eyes and voice were soft. He felt safe instinctively but didn't know why. Maybe it was surrender. She slowly draped the halter over his neck. He sighed and followed her to her barn.

There they were, buzzing around in their little tractor. The Barn Owners (BO's). It's feeding time and they are carrying alfalfa, mash, and Bermuda pellets with all the horses giving them their attention as they zoom down the stall aisles, the horses are whinnying and pacing. Snickers receives his pellets and they pour water on them. His teeth were discovered to be so worn down he could not chew hay. No one knew he wasn't getting enough food for who knows how long! Finally, he is calming down, filling out, his coat is shinier and his demeanor a bit less aloof, not quite friendly yet but not angry anymore. His owner accepts my advice and offering of supplements. She says "you can ride him anytime". I leapt at that chance. However, after having only brief reentry into horseback riding at the age of 59 after a 30-year gap, my riding skills were almost non-existent at best and at worst, unbalanced! After his grooming sessions improved, his lunge work improved, I finally tack him up for the inaugural ride. Trying on several different saddles and bridles I settle on a nice English all-purpose saddle with an English hackamore. He seems to appreciate not having a bit in his mouth with those teeth issues. We ride around in the round pen first. His tongue hangs out. Kind of his "signature" look. I assume it's due to his teeth that he can't keep his tongue in but it's noticeably longer and flapping out of his mouth when I ride. The little girls in the riding program point and laugh at him. I notice he's "off" on his front left (the hoof he refuses to pick up). We just walk. His shoulder falls in not wanting to bend when we turn right. We walk on out of the round pen and attempt to walk around the property. It's a beautiful Spring day. We visit the other horses, walking and enjoying. I steer him to the arena. There are poles on the ground left from a prior rider. Snickers takes a beeline for them! I'll be! This horse HAD to have been a former jumper. I learn more about him every day. We pretend to jump over (we WALKED over the pole!). I praise him up. He's so proud of himself you'd think he just jumped a four foot oxer!

The BO's drive by and stop. Handing me a letter, they say, "well we got your letter, so here's ours." I open it and read. All the blood feels like it has drained out of my body and I am in shock. "…this is a private facility…." "…do not attempt to advertise any business of yours in reference to this facility…" "…There are plenty of other larger facilities that would welcome your volunteering"… Previously there had been notice to the boarders (of which I was NOT one) cautioning about running businesses and the resultant liability it may pose to the ranch owners. I meticulously explained in my letter to them in attempts to appease the BO's concerns that ***I volunteered*** working with the different horses there (after taking lessons from their trainer). The boarders approached me, not me approaching them. I refused to take money. They liked the way I worked with their horses and asked me to care for them as they went on vacation. I also was doing Equine Massage and energy work and offered a certificate of insurance protecting them from any liability of my offering my services there. But nope, I was being given the 'boot'! I was crushed! I'd been there for a year after that day Spirit poked me on the shoulder and shouted in my ear urging my destiny on to this place. I'd gotten to know so many great friends and horses, and I had just bonded with Snickers. What could I do? I couldn't LIVE without him!

Snickers had already said it....***Change, nothing stays the same!***

It's Cloudy

The woman placed pine shavings in the stall. She fixed his hay net and his water bucket so he could easily reach. The other horses were sniffing and shifting their weight to see him. He saw their beautiful shining coats and their well-manicured hooves. If he were a human, he'd be embarrassed at his looks. It was as if he was transported from a time when he looked like them and now was a homeless man, dirty and disheveled and not belonging here. No one would remember him as he was. Shining and strong. He drank with intent on the clear clean water. He tried to eat the hay she left. It clumped in his mouth and he dropped it out into a pile onto the floor. It looked like a rats nest on the floor. He could taste the loveliness of the grass with a bit of the juice from his chewing on it but he couldn't swallow. He nodded off, still hungry but hopeful and periodically watching out the barn window as the puffy clouds rolled out to sunset.

"You should ride her! You can ride her anytime!" Sylvia was sitting on her white Welsh Pony mare as the mare was prancing, backing up and generally being naughty. Yeah right! I think as I just smile at her and her old mare. I'm at the trainer's barn tacking up for a trail ride – a nice treat the trainer throws in every occasionally, for my helping her with the horses. That horse is jumpy and anxious, I will never be good enough to ride her I think to myself. My lessons were progressing with a lot of "heels down", "elbows", "Post! up/down, up/down". I feel like an awkward lump as I can barely post the trot without holding on. Wow, how did I do this in my twenties so easily? Thirty years and thirty pounds ago!

How it happened down the road, I don't know but Sylvia was persistent as she followed me in my lessons and as I was progressing she kept encouraging me. "You should ride her" she would say in her Austrian accent. I don't even remember the first time I did finally ride that pony. It went ok. Several times I was tacking her up and a tree branch would fall "BLAM!" there she went – crazy mare pulls right away from the tie. I decided to use my skills on her with essential oils. "Ah, lavender should calm her down" I think. BLAM! She pulls away from my hands from the scent of what was supposed to be a calming experience like I was going to kill her.

Ignorance is bliss as they say. I want more of a training experience and Sylvia and I are sneaking off to the next-door barn with her mare where there is a Dressage trainer. Lunge lessons go ok first couple times even though the anxious mare is calling out to her friends and is obviously stressed just walking over there.

Today was ominous. I felt the strike of the letter that was delivered by the BO's the day before. I felt my stomach churning. I felt like I was trespassing on their property and my little voice was telling me "maybe this isn't a day for a lesson on that skittish old mare". I ignore my inner voice. I must walk over alone and Sylvia meets me there at the Dressage barn off the property of the BO's. The mounting block was stacked with saddles and tack where we normally would mount. For some reason, Sylvia keeps leaving me to go look at the other lesson going on. I look and see another mounting block by the hunter/jumper arena and head over there. I line up with the block, but the old mare is obviously prancy. I just tell myself, if I just quickly get on, it'll all be ok. I have one foot in the stirrup, I start to throw my right leg over and I feel her shaking, prancing and moving. It was as if she was "quaking" ready to explode. In a split-second decision, I say to myself "NO,

I'll jump off her now rather than risk my neck in a bolt." Ah, YES! I land on both feet square on the ground. Ah, NOOOOO, one second later my leg buckles, mare running off, I've lost the reins and watch her run home as I know without a doubt as I lay on the ground my leg is broken.

Six Weeks

He was running, prancing, tossing his head. The others just watched with amusement. He thought to himself how so many weeks ago, he would not have had any energy to be doing this. After the woman's kindness and care, his coat was again shinier, his legs felt strong and his eyes were clear and bright. The Ferrier had shaped his feet a few times already. The woman finally figured out his teeth were so bad, he couldn't chew hay. She made him a delicious mash of pellets and water and grain. He was indeed an older horse but he felt strong and looked younger than his years. The little girl at the barn occasionally would sneak him treats of carrot pieces that he still was able to chew. He was happy!

The hospital stay was long. Only a few days but seemed long to me. Surgery went well on the broken tibia and fibula with a rod in place. It was determined the mare had struck me with her hoof as she bolted off. I was kicked right in the tibia and the snap I felt was my fibula breaking as the tibia was no longer supporting my leg. Visitors gave me their stories of their own "war wounds" from riding accidents. All I could think of is how long it would be before I could see Snickers again.

It was probably two weeks after the surgery that I begged Sue to PLEASE take me to see Snickers. I sat in the car next to his stall. He seemed angry again. His coat was duller. He ignored me. I cried.

Finally, after a few more weeks I forced myself to drive even though I was on a cane and hobbling horribly and still in pain. I hobbled into the round pen with intention as Sue brought Snickers in. Snickers lunged himself around me in his prancy gait blowing "dragon snorts". It was as if he knew I was vulnerable and could not possibly be his leader right now. I was crushed. All the work we strived for. All the progress we made with our rides. How long would it take? Patience was never my strong suit!

The ground at the ranch was so uneven and soft. The BO's choose to "drag" the property, moving more and more manure into the soil, it just churned it up into a soft loam. My foot and ankle could barely stand in it. I'm standing at Snickers stall with my cane when the BO comes over and barks "WHY do you do this?" I explain "It's in my blood. Can't help it, it's a horse addiction disease I guess" I smile meekly. He glares at me and says "you need to leave, you are a liability!" I glare back. "I've never sued anyone and don't plan to. I realize riding is at my own risk". I'm confused. My injury didn't even take place on HIS property! He obviously wants me gone. I ask him with teary eyes and a closed throat "what about him?" pointing to Snickers. "I have fallen in love with him!". He mumbles and looks down and says he would talk to the other (female) BO and jets off on his tractor. Typical man that won't stand up to a teary-eyed woman! I'm left feeling doomed. I plan to "buy" Snickers and hope that he and I can then stay.

I share my plan the next day. "NO! How dare you, you can't just assume you can buy him and stay here!" The BO is obviously not understanding the love bond Snickers and I have. I stutter, "Well of course I was going to ask you after I worked it out with Sue". Something or someone was at work here. I kept wondering what I had done wrong? Who hates me? I was obviously a point of contention for them and it wasn't going to be negotiable or resolved at any time. I went home, got drunk and cried myself to sleep as I realized the horrid reality was I would never be able to see Snickers again!

Change is good

She came to his stall as usual in the morning. She was talking into that black square thing again. What WAS that! She always had it. It must be food he thought. "Yes, he's perfect for a companion horse". "Yes, he's older but he would be great. He gets along well with the others. Your baby horse needs a teacher/companion. Of course, I'll be here. Come take a look". The other woman came and looked at him. She was pretty. Long blonde hair with sparkly blue eyes. He felt her presence was somewhat awkward. Like she didn't really understand where to put her feet and hands. "Awe, he's so cute. I'll take him". Another truck rumbled up the drive. Snickers feet felt the vibration and again he had a pit in his stomach. He wasn't hungry. He was scared. Change again. Nothing stays the same.

After days of missing him and deeply heartbroken I begin to look for other barns I could move him to. I find several. Sue accompanies me and we settle on a cute barn not too far away. I'm scared of owning him on my own. I'm afraid of taking him away from all his friends – and missing mine! I already feel lonely, missing my former life with my barn friends. After the move to the new barn, Snickers settles into his routine and falls in love with his next-door neighbor, a senior Arabian mare with a skinny body and perpetually cocked tail. My foot is still a problem two months later after the accident but I hobble around in the barn and the arena with him. He almost holds me up sometimes when we walk. The new BO is nice. She's into "natural care" for the animals so we bond that way.

We begin to ride again. Riding is scary. My stomach flutters with butterflies, my hands break out in sweat and my legs are like rubber when I mount. It's easier to ride than to walk however – the stirrups not as painful on my foot as the pressure of walking.

Snickers becomes progressively more and more spooky. Sue visits often and videos our rides. Snickers is doing a "side step" spook at the various corners. She remarks on how he never did that before. I remember his spooks being just a little hop. These were getting bigger. I remark that an old horse like this has probably "been there/done that" and has seen most things so he should not be so afraid.

Several months go by. I am riding periodically. He runs at the trot with his head up. Trying to get it over with. I wonder if his arthritis is bothering him. Today, my friends are coming by to see us ride. I'm warming him up in the arena. I am relaxed, we are walking around pretty much aimless when I feel him shudder, shake and then it's a blur. Snickers is across the full arena after a "duck and buck". It felt like a small slow motion buckaroo rodeo. "Whoah! No! Ok, (resolved) here I go again – I'm coming off to the right side, just try to land well!" I tell myself and then…Thump! I'm down on my butt. I look up from the ground relieved I'm only bruised, not broken this time. I look at my saddle which was completely off the right side of Snickers as he's gazing down at me with that "hey, what r you doing down there?" look. I stayed on pretty well until that last moment! Darn fleece girth! I congratulate myself and am wiping off the dirt as my friends are approaching. Snickers is still sketchy about his "scary corner". We walk over to get the boogey man gone. I fix the tack, remount and walk a few paces to show him I'm boss! My hands are sweaty and the bruise on my butt is numb and getting swollen. I must fly out the next day. Damn! Sitting in that airplane is going to be hard to do!

I remove his grain and alfalfa from his feedings to lessen any of his "hotness". I have the vet out to check his eyes. Looks fine there. I change saddles. My BO says it's because he doesn't see me as his leader. I balk at that. She is increasingly getting on my nerves with her "know it all attitude".

Up up and away!

The mare was the matriarch of the barn. She was not the oldest on the property (that was Snickers!) but she was the "alpha" mare. All the horses looked up to her as their leader. They whinnied whenever she moved from her stall to the arena. The vet was out at 10AM that day. The BO felt her mare had not been "quite right" for a few days and now, the mare was pacing, picking at her sides and sweating profusely. This was not good! She had been saved from a very bad laminitis attack five years earlier. The BO had been very careful about feed making sure it was low sugar, excellent quality grass and no treats. Now, it was hard to watch as her mare was obviously in a very bad colic state. Hourly the barn boarders that were there watched her and took turns rubbing her and scratching her favorite scratch spots to relax her. The vet arrived, took her vitals and sent the tube down her nostrils all the way into the stomach. In went the oil, water and magnesium solution. All we could do was wait, pray and try to keep her comfortable. Finally, hours after the vet left -a poop! A great sign! Although the balls of poop

were dry and with mucus, it may mean that the mare could start to clear the impaction. She seemed less stressed, the sweat dried, but she continued to turn circles, reflux liquid from her nostrils continued to flow out on occasion and she would paw the ground periodically.

2:30AM, the BO went out to check on her…she was gone. The matriarch had passed. It was as if she waited for everyone to leave her to her peace at hand. She was ready to go on up to Rainbow Bridge…

Sue looked up to the ceiling, transporting herself away. "Up up and away" she repeated silently to herself while he violated her innocence. It's been happening for a while. He would come to her after drinking. He always said she was his special little girl. She smelled the strong whiff of alcohol on his breathe and felt the weight of his body as he lifted her nightie. She wanted to puke. She left the space she was in and would not remember. Up up and away she would go with other thoughts than what was the unspeakable. She couldn't tell her Mom. Her Mom would send her away. She resolved to be better. Maybe if she was more quiet and less outspoken. Maybe if she wasn't so pretty with her long blond hair. Yes, that's it! I'll cut it in the morning she thought. I just won't be a girl anymore!

Before school she went to the barn, didn't bother with the saddle and just climbed on Missy with a halter and rode out into the Texas morning sunshine. She rode and rode, tears streaming down. She rode until she didn't remember. Missy was a fractious horse. She tried to run anyone riding her into any pole or object she could find. This morning Missy ran off with Sue to the gas station across the street where she nearly lost her head from having to duck under the sign. She loved this horse. She loved the freedom and the wind in her now short hair.

Years went by and he lost interest as she got older. She still went to that place. "Up up and away" she would go whenever she had pressure from the guys on dates. They teased her and called her a cold fish. She didn't care. She had Missy. When she rode, it was freedom and she didn't feel a care in the world. Her mom was a nurse. She would care for people and be like her Mom. Then maybe he would love her again.

Baby Horses

He stood near his mother's belly, his nose nestled close in. Suddenly there was movement in the barn. A sharp pungent smell permeated his nostrils. He felt his mother shift and then prance in the stall but every once in a while, reaching down to push him under close to her belly. There was shouting and a lot of noise when the barn doors opened. His mother's head was high and she was yelling like he's never heard her yell before. It was a panicked look he saw in her eyes. Her eyes showed their whites and her head was held high and her nostrils larger than he can remember seeing. Suddenly the adrenaline surged through him as he also felt her panic. The smell was strong and it suffocated the air with dryness. He could barely take in a breath as his nostrils flared and he coughed. Trailers were lining the barn entrance. "Take them first", "we have to leave NOW" the humans were yelling and he could sense their panic as well. His mother was coughing and yelling and coughing. She remembered him and occasionally pushed him close to her belly. This was different than when the shows were going and his

mother was stressed and there was a lot of chaos with the humans at the barn. This was different and he could tell it was serious. Suddenly someone threw a halter on his mother and pulled her out of the stall. She was prancing and he could hear her hooves loudly clapping the concrete floor. There was so much commotion and people running everywhere he didn't know what to do but decided to run after his mother trying to keep up. They were loaded onto the trailer and suddenly hauled away. He saw a bright orange light just over the hill where he and his mother had grazed only yesterday. Safety awaited down the road – Snickers was safe.

He loaded into the trailer with trepidation but curious about the other horse in there. He looked small and light colored. He was wiggling. Can a horse "wiggle"? This one seemed like he just could not stand still. Snickers sniffed at him as he climbed in next to the baby horse in the trailer and the small horse wheeled around and tried to bite at him. Oh, boy good thing for the trailer separation gates. As they off loaded into the pasture, the baby horse ran out and bucked a few times and snaked his neck around. He charged right at Snickers. Snickers made a quick duck away and opened his mouth and charged right back at the baby horses rear end. I don't have the time for these games he thought. "Ooooh, good", Sue praised Snickers. "You will be a good teacher". She turned and left him alone with the swirling dervish of a baby horse. He slept well that night. He was tired but hungry. The baby horse ate the hay and the pasture grass but Snickers was again dropping the "rat's nests" back into the hay bin. As he tried hard to gain some nourishment out of the hay she left them, it just got covered up and the hay molded and smelled. The woman put new hay on top of the old the next day and commented on his lack of appetite, shrugged and let them both out to the pasture. "Here ya go, maybe you will like the fresh grass outside better". He felt the hunger and the anger well up in his stomach.

"I don't know why he's losing so much weight". Maybe the new surroundings?". Sue lamented about Snickers dull coat, bony hips and angry demeanor to her friend. The baby must be running him around a lot she surmised.

Snickers bit her on the arm and stomped his foot at feeding time. He would not let her near his head. He was trying so very hard to tell her about his food. She was still awkward and not listening. He was angry and hungry. Couldn't she see?

The dentist came. "Well, Sue, this horse is not 24, he's at least 30 given the condition of his teeth". "He can't chew hay – he quids and could choke. You must give him pellets with water in order for him to receive any nourishment". Sue contemplated the old horse. She had climbed on him bareback a few times and rode the property. He once ran into a fence he apparently didn't see. He had tripped a few times. She realized she had been asking a lot of this horse at his age. He was truly just a companion to her baby horse who was proceeding to become larger and unrulier by the day. Baby horse was rearing and she was afraid of him. She refused to pick up their feet lest she be kicked the way she was with her grandfather's horse when she was young. Snickers tolerated the baby horse. It was a job. It was unnerving and tiresome but he did it well. It was better than some of his past. He tried not to remember. Up up and away he thought.

Fences and Feelings

He was electrified. He felt the rider surge him on and he took the cue. Galloping faster now, the rider pulled on his mouth to slow him up right before the fence. There! Riders leg goes on, heels go down and the hands forward giving away the reins. He planted his hind legs into a spring. They made it with room to spare and the rider crashed down on his back. Again, he rounded the corner where the rider pointed him. The fences were getting bigger. His knees felt like they were going to buckle under him. At the last minute, he shied away and refused the fence. The crowd let out a low moan. The disappointment could be felt through the riders' hands and legs. He knew. Snickers was done with his jumping career.

She admired herself in the mirror. Smart jacket, the latest breeches and her hair was pulled back in a tight low bun with a black bow just below the helmet. She had been riding all her life. There was nothing that scared her. Her thoroughbred gelding was a pill. He would not work for anyone but her. She knew his vices and his tricks. He was not to get away with anything. -especially today! Stella pulled on her boots and took one last approving look before leaving the tack room. She mounted Casper quickly and confidently. She gave him no time to think about the lights, the flags the banners, or the sounds of the crowd that was giving him the nerves. She rode confidently but harshly using her crop every chance she thought he may hesitate or spook. Her legs were strong. She pushed him on and they began the course. First cantering around, eyeing the fence layout. She had walked it earlier in the day and noted the large oxer after a tight turn left. Casper's weaker side was going left. But then they began. One over the other, Stella pushed him on then pulled him back right before the jump. Her heels went down and her hands forward, her legs wrapped lightly but firmly around his barrel. Her face looked determined. Casper caught her feeling as a contagiousness in adrenaline and sheer will. His determination came from her. They made the course with no faults and time to spare. Stella thumped his neck and beamed as they exited the arena. They were first! The way Stella preferred everything. She had to be number one. She had to win.

Who's Training Who

It was one of those nights where you are so exhausted, you almost go into what I call "zombie" mode. Make dinner, make lunches for the morning, shower, brush teeth… Being a full time career woman, wife, Mom to a second grader and trying to keep up with my health as a runner was taking its toll. I looked in on my husband sleeping and climbed into bed hoping he is as exhausted as me! I just don't have it in me tonight for the "wifey duty". I drift off and dream…I saw the most vivid colors and felt the most depth of feelings I've ever known a dream to have. I was in a most beautiful meadow on a spectacular white horse. It was whiter than white and the meadow a myriad of brilliant greens, yellows and white. Words can't do justice to the colors or the feelings. It sounds so cliché like a movie but it was the feelings of LOVE that were so intense. Happiness that I cannot describe in earthly terms filled my soul. I awoke disappointed. I didn't want to 'come back'. That feeling stayed with me all day going to work.

I just wanted to go back to that place and with that horse…with those feelings of love and happiness. It must have been I was in heaven!

The spooking continued. Snickers could barely be walked around the property without seeing a boogeyman. It seemed there was a horse eating leaf around every corner! He had his "scary corners" in the arena. It was my last hope. I watched as my new BO was lunging her horse. She seemed to have finesse and confidence. Her horse was young and green. I knew the history there. She got her from a woman who had just left her to pasture. No one had ridden her. She was a redheaded mare. Like an Irish temper, she let it be known, she didn't want to go around this stupid person on this stupid rope. My BO just laughed at her and went with her as she ran away bucking. Eventually the horse settled and it seemed they were in a dance. Going one way and then gracefully turning to the other direction

I decided to bite my pride and ask for help with Snickers. We began. He ran. And ran and ran. Only to the left! I could not get him to turn. He was a stubborn rascal. He refused to turn. This was not the graceful dance I saw with BO with her horse. I stood there and decided to be quiet. Wait it out. Eventually he would be tired but I always worry about this old horse getting injured. He was getting lathered up with stress. Suddenly I had a slight flicker of his ear. I stole the chance and walked in front of him pointing the other direction with the lunge rope and raising the whip aside the air next to his cheek on the left. He finally conceded and quickly jumped and turned right. I dropped the whip, went up to him and scratched his neck and we were done. Things were different from there. He had finally acknowledged me as his leader.

To understand a horse's need for leadership and how that lends to their feeling of safety was an enlightenment for me. I continued to learn and practice. Snickers became stronger physically and more mentally alert. He loved to learn! Here was this old horse having fun learning and was so pleased with himself when he did well. Our relationship flourished. I was "dancing" with him eventually off the lunge line. We would play in the arena. He would run and buck and play. He would come to me and we would trot and canter in a circle. He would yield his hindquarters and his front legs. We worked on some tricks. He loves to bow for treats. He and I are a team!

Transferring the ground work to riding took a bit of relearning on my part. This form of "natural horsemanship" required me to ride him with a loose rein and NO steering to start out. I no longer tried to put him into a frame. I had to have his attention on this loose rein (with NO bit) and learned to turn him so he would yield his head to me and yield his hindquarters. This became a routine for us and to this day he almost starts doing it before I ask! Eventually, I started bringing him back to a frame (he got immediately nervous again with his head flying up in the air so it took time and releasing him to the loose rein and trying again). Then we started doing some shoulder in, leg yields and low and behold, I see this boy must have had some Dressage training! Again, I learn about Mr. Snickers! He loves to tell me our routine. Don't dare forget the turn on the hunches over at the mirror. He will remind me!

Nothing Stays the Same

Stella's horse was throwing his head, pacing back and forth and had thrown a shoe. He was in a larger stall than most of the horses as he was a good 17 plus hand high thoroughbred. He was literally "pitching a fit". I saw him pointing to his sides with his nose occasionally and thought the worst. Colic looks like this.

I didn't really know Stella. I'd seen her a few times and went on a trail ride with her and her niece once. She always seemed aloof and like she could care less to remember me. I got her phone number and called. I let her know about her horse. I suggested she may want to call the vet (and the Ferrier due to his shoe). What followed in conversation was a scolding like no other. Every other word from her was "F" this or "F" that! Don't EVER say vet she yelled into the phone at me. I was flabbergasted. Why would this woman be mad about me letting her know about her horse pitching a fit and potentially falling to colic? We didn't get off on the right foot.

I told my other friends she was as nutty and neurotic as her horse! I wanted nothing to do with her. My one friend stated she'd known Stella for almost twenty years and she was as kind hearted as they come and she was extremely knowledgeable about horses. Well I'm one to give the benefit of the doubt. In interest of keeping the peace around the place, somehow, I found a way to approach her and apologize, realizing I may have upset her at work with the news about her horse.

As I found, Stella was kind and loving on the inside although always aloof and came of somewhat "snooty" on the outside. We became fast friends. We were shopping at a local tack shop when she mentioned she had her mammogram come back questionable. She was worried but she was stoic. She had experienced a cancer with lymphoma some twenty years prior. It was back.

As we bantered joking and laughing about little things in the waiting room prior to surgery, it was as if she was going to get her tonsils out. We were in denial. Then I said good bye as they wheeled my friend into surgery to remove her breast. We both cried.

Chemo was new to her. She had radiation previously so to have another radiation treatment may be risky. She underwent chemo like a champ. She was tired, she was hurting but she had a smile on her face most days. She liked her bald head, her beanies and losing weight. She joked. She did not go see her horse – for a YEAR! I don't know how one does that. She didn't want to upset him she said. Said she'd be too emotional. Others pitched in and took care of him. He lost weight. He got angry. He was pissed off when she went to see him for the first time. He got over it. She made it through chemo and proton therapy radiation but not without breaking her leg while sorting laundry. Back into the hospital she went. She couldn't come home for months. She wasn't afraid to ask for help. That was surprising about Stella. This stoic woman of a perfectionist nature. She wanted the help and appreciated it and asked when she needed it.

I remember him asking, "My friend has a son out there. A place in "the ranch" area. His son is a contractor, do you know him perhaps?" I laughed. "Grandpa, it's a very big city here. There are so many people. I would have no idea who he is or how to find him." My grandfather remembered me when I was younger whenever we visited them on Long Island. He knew how "horse crazy" I was and made sure to call his neighbor Nancy to see if I could visit her and her horse. Nancy was usually too busy to have me along but every once in a while, I could watch her in her lessons. Grandpa passed at 92. I'm pretty sure he was looking down on me with his friend with the contractor son up there in heaven and somehow connected me with "C" and the rescue ranch!

The rescue ranch was in an upscale rural area of the county where windy roads and large lots with mansions and "horse property" coexisted amongst large Eucalyptus trees and a smattering of golf courses. The bicyclists took their life in their hands to ride the narrow streets just for the scenery. It was an escape away from the busy city - an oasis away from traffic and the concrete jungle. It was an unusual place for a horse rescue but it was a sanctuary to the horses as well as us volunteers. The peacefulness was broken by the bark of the owner. “Hey! Get them over there. I said NOT to put the mares out yet. What are you doing!”. She was exasperated and it showed. The new volunteer cringed under the criticism. It was as if she played a game to see how much she could belittle the “newbies” and make them feel small. She was a tiny thing about 4’11” and 90lbs dripping wet and looked like a jockey and in fact had worked at the track exercising the race horses at one time. For as tiny as she was, she was “scrappy”. You can’t rescue horses without having a heart for them but for people sometimes we wondered. Catherine (we called her “C”) never married, didn’t have children or a current boyfriend and as far as everyone could tell her only passion was the horses. Whenever I wanted to learn something new, it was difficult to get by her obvious joy in belittling my incapable old body. “You don’t approach their feet like you are picking up a stump!”, “Slouch down more” “You look like a stickman” “You can’t ride, I don’t allow that ‘centered riding’ stuff here”. She wanted to transform my upright form ingrained from the Dressage work many years ago, into a western cowboy look.

Once, when we went to her brother's house in the nearby neighborhood, she handed him a wad of cash like I've never seen in my life. I looked away uncomfortable. I didn't know their arrangement and I never asked questions. They were born and bred New York Italians and he was a contractor that drove a Maserati. I knew she was filed as a non-profit for the horse rescue. That next month, there were ladies sitting in her kitchen obviously "going through the books". A month later, there was a new person on the Board. Things seemed to change. The house needed a new roof. It got done. They needed a new tractor which was never affordable previously and it appeared. The efforts to rescue new horses was increased. The original 15 horses on the property were never really up for adoption during the years I was there. It seemed it was possible to keep horses there only for C's own pleasure. How else could she afford a mansion property in "the ranch".

I knew way too much about her "horse business". Our relationship became even more strained as she targeted me and set me up for ridicule at every opportunity. I eventually left but continued to support the horse rescue efforts.

Healing

The patient was obviously in no pain. He had suffered a severe stroke. The monitor showed his vitals and he was as stable as he could be. Sue wondered where the neurologist was. She had rung him due to the obvious signs of increased edema. She would need his attendance to reduce the swelling to prevent further damage to this patient's brain. Since the opening of the new hospital things weren't as they used to be. As a critical care nurse, you need to be able to easily see and get to your patients. The new critical care wing (the "Cruise Ship" as staffers referred to it) was not physically laid out to be conducive to care. She had only left this patient a few minutes and upon return discovered the signs of edema. The family waited anxiously outside the room. She paced the room, adjusting the bed, making sure the vitals were accurately monitored. Suddenly the monitor alarmed. The neurologist entered the room. The patient experienced a massive stroke and subsequent heart attack and dies quickly. Sue is devastated knowing the family was counting on her care. She is devastated that yet again, the MD's can't get there fast enough. Where was this guy anyway? Out to dinner at his wife's fancy parties again. There was no sense of urgency like the old days in medical care. She supposed the machine was supposed to keep her patient alive for his highnesses convenience?!

The following day Sue was summoned to administration. The office was nice and appointed with spa like furniture and overlooked a serenity garden of rocks and succulents. It was peace in the storm. "I'm sorry Sue, this is the second time". The words were barely audible as Sues blood pressure rose. They were doing it again!? How dare they! They are accusing her of malpractice? She followed protocol to the letter. Where was the neurologist in this? Likely he beat her to it and decided to cover his own ass. "We are letting you know you are on probation and asking you to reduce your duties to that of floor nurse". Again, it was stinging so hard, her ears barely heard and her heart was in her mouth. Thirty-five years of this. I've been an impeccable worker, supervisor, training all the newbies here.

Devastated, she returned home, poured herself a few glasses (or more) of wine and cried herself to sleep. All she wanted to do was see Baby Horse. He was grown, out of control with his rearing but she needed him. Being out there at the ranch calmed her. She could leave all the nastiness of the hospital politics be behind her.

She was unusually tired and felt a tingling in her arm. It was a burning sensation. At first, she thought she had tweaked it with raucous Baby Horse maneuvers. No, she was an experienced nurse and knew the signs. She was having signs of a Heart Attack! “Noooo, I’m too young. My god!” She had Robert take her in immediately to the ER. Yes, the Cath lab she knew all too well was in on the visit. She had experienced a mild heart attack. The cardiologist explained that heart disease/failure is fundamentally caused by a deficiency in the parasympathetic nervous system. The known things that nourish our parasympathetic nervous system are: contact with nature, loving relations, trust, economic security and sex! In other words, her heart was broken. She was so stressed by the reprimands and probation, she suffered a response physically from the emotional toll.

Weeks went by and she consulted with the union rep. “Better to resign Sue than let them let you go”. Sue resigned. She spent every day at the ranch “nurturing her heart”. She still worried so much about what happened at the job and not having a job and money and how would she find another job and what would Robert feel about her not contributing. But she did have to admit if this all had not happened, she wouldn't be experiencing less stress and the nurturing that she had at the ranch. Her health was just more important right now.

"Yes, this is Sue". She lost all color from her face as she heard the person on the other end of the phone speak. She could not speak, felt her knees go weak and she could not be sure of her feelings. "Yes, thank you". She hung up the phone. Robert was watching her closely. They had too close of a call with her heart attack not too long ago. "What's up?" he asked her. "Dad died" she answered and turned away with no emotion.

She lay in bed looking up at the ceiling not sure of her feelings. She was glad he was dead. He was a sick, mean and nasty person. He had hurt her. Mom had died years before leaving her a legacy of a small inheritance amount. She wanted nothing from him. Why was she angry? Up up and away she thought as she dozed and dreamt of other things. Baby horse, please stop rearing.

Spring Eternal

“Hands down, elbows bent. That it! Now bring her in a bit. Good!” The training was progressing well. The mare was older and experienced and the trainer constantly assuring me she had “never bucked” (famous last words I thought!). I was ‘cheating’ on my regular trainer. While riding Dressage again now for almost a year, I still hadn’t cantered and leg yielded or done shoulder in (at least when I tried my trainer would scoff and say “well, it wasn’t IT!” and we’d have to go back to walk/trot transitions -again and STILL!) I know my injured past. I know my old body doesn’t bounce like it used to but I know my seat and balance have developed well through my regular training. This new trainer was more accommodating and encouraging to trying things I’ve not done (or at least hadn’t done for a looong time!). I was having fun. The mare wasn’t as easy to canter as my old boy Snickers. Imagine that! Old Boy Snickers beating this ole girl who was maybe 10 years his junior. “Caaaanterrrr” she yelled, “Caaanterrr” I pleaded but pop she would start with throwing me out of the saddle and I immediately posted. Argh! This is nuts.

My brain just can't seem to get it. Finally, one last loop to the left (on her and my good side). And "Caaaanterrr" and we were there. I remember the magical rocking horse feeling as I moved with the horse and softened my back yet kept my core stable and legs long. "Beautiful" she yelled. And we ended a beautiful lesson with me panting out of breath but happy.

Tacking Snickers up has become easier over the years. He used to prance around, jut his head at me and generally move off right at the moment you needed him to be still. He wouldn't tie at ALL! Now, I can walk him through the "tunnel" between the tack rooms and the pond with the loud honking geese to the wash rack, tie him and he stays perfectly content. Treats and more treats have shown him it's a good place to be. A treat for picking up your feet, A treat for girthing up and not biting, A treat for getting your bridle on. The air was perfect and I sensed an air of calmness with Snickers today. We were both enjoying the grooming and tacking up. The geese were even quiet for a change as they used their little play pool to groom and bathe. He watched patiently as I donned my helmet after stuffing my hair up. Bringing over his bit less bridle, he ducked his head down to help me put it on. It's been years since a bit has been in his mouth. He does just fine without one. We walk toward the arena and he does his usual obligatory stop (like "I don't want to go") but a gentle nudge of the reins and he's moving with me again. I choose not to lunge him with the tack on as I'd been doing recently. It seems to be a nice cool day. I wondered if he may be a little "fresh" and spunky today. Lately he's been a bit slow and reluctant to pick up the trot. Definitely not like him. I used to THINK trot and he'd go. I'd have to use outside rein to get him to stop running through it and collect a bit but he'd at least go. Lately, he was a bit off and slow.

We do our usual routine. After treats for "whoa" at the mounting block, I mount. I yield his head to right, then to the left. Walk off a bit and then yield hindquarters to the right then to the left. Move off in walk at loose rein. Bug him if he stops or is "destination driven" at the gate. He always seems so very old and slow to start. I worry about him tripping or me hurting him if I push him too much. We got through the rainy season and he didn't get much exercise as our arena was like a pool most of the winter. I'm concerned about overdoing too soon.

As I pick him up on the walk, he seems to have more pep but no spook. A good day indeed. We do a bit of shoulder fore at his "spooky" areas of the arena. He calms right down and we do a bit of leg yield to the right – his favorite maneuver! Circle to the top and face the mirror. Another one of his favorite, turn on the haunches and we walk to the right. His hard side is going right yet he seems he's picking up some flexibility and strength. He's not falling into the arena as much as he used to. He's not as stressed as I move him toward his scary corner in the shoulder fore to the right. We circle round and I ask for the trot. He barely trots, it's more of a shuffle. I urge him on with my posting rhythm and my "cluck" "cluck" "cluck" that he likes to hear to keep a beat. We do some sitting trot then I urge him forward again. Trying trot to the right is disastrous as always. I don't know what ever happened to this poor guy. I wish I knew his history but he's' totally atrophied on the right. His right knee kind of splays outward. Likely a jumping accident.

We 'round the corner and I talk to him out loud. "Ok bud, we haven't cantered in a while. Your trot seems slow so once I get you in a good rhythm we are going to try today ok? You ready?" He seems to understand as his ears prick back to me and forward again. An ever so slight move of his head, we trot around the corner, I scoop my inner seat bone on the left, move my right heel back and ‘kiss’ the air. He smoothly scoops me up into a rhythmic and strong left lead canter. We only go a half circle and I ask for trot again. He takes his time and slowly descends to trot. Nice transition! Not his usual clunk to a trot movement. This boy is a senior wonder! I smile and giggle and throw my arms around his neck. “GOOD BOY” I effuse. He’s the best horse in the whole world to me. He looks at me with a blasé eye as if to say “So, what’s the big fuss?” He is beaming though. He loves doing good work. Then he does his bow with his right leg bent and his head down

patiently awaiting his treat. Well done!

The barn is cool in the shade, yet hot in the sun. I pick half sun and half shade to eat my lunch. I was famished after riding and chores with no breakfast and it was already after 2PM. After settling my sandwich down at the table beyond the arena I had a full view of Snickers. Good I thought, I can watch my boy and enjoy my lunch. It’s rare but special when I have the barn to myself. No one else around, late afternoon Sunday and a perfect puffy cloud day of 68 degrees.

I finish my sandwich and fries (hmmm need to watch that but boy was I hungry!) and walk over to the chairs in the sun. It's been awhile since I've just 'sat'. I mean just 'sat' and done nothing. Observe. I watched puffy clouds and their shadows over the pond. I soak in the sun's rays and appreciate the warmth. The ducks are trying to nest over on the roof of the tack room. The air is still and quiet. I listen. The horses are quiet, most of them napping. It is a lovely end to a day. I moved over to Snickers' stall before leaving. He has his back to me facing the corner. His usual napping pose. He sees me and saunters over. I'm tired and want a nap too. I put my arms crossed on the stall door and lay my head down. He gently nuzzles my arm and sniffs and blows his horse breathe on me softly. We both hang our heads and slightly nod off.

-END-

Art by Lauren Howard©

www.ingramcontent.com/pod-product-compliance
Ingram Content Group UK Ltd.
Pitfield, Milton Keynes, MK11 3LW, UK
UKHW041916190726
13854UKWH00003B/1276